5-Minute Fairytale Stories

by Robert Rudman and Ellie Rose

Little, Brown and Company

New York ✳ Boston

Cover design by Carolyn Bull.

Little, Brown and Company
Hachette Book Group
1290 Avenue of the Americas, New York, NY 10104
Visit us at LBYR.com
everafterhigh.com

First Edition: October 2017

Little, Brown and Company is a division of Hachette Book Group, Inc.
The Little, Brown name and logo are trademarks of Hachette Book Group, Inc.

Library of Congress Control Number 2017935528

ISBNs: 978-0-316-54816-8 (paper over board), 978-0-316-44483-5 (ebook),
978-0-316-44481-1 (ebook), 978-0-316-44484-2 (ebook)

Printed in China

APS

10 9 8 7 6 5 4 3 2 1

Table of Contents

Raven Queen

The Ever After High "Book-to-School" orientation was the week before classes started, and the Charmitorium was packed with everyone telling tales about their summers.

But there was also another story being told....

There was hexcitement in the air, because this year everyone was going to pledge his or her destiny to the Storybook of Legends during Legacy Day. Raven Queen, the daughter of the Evil Queen, sat next to Madeline Hatter, daughter of the Mad Hatter and Raven's best friend forever after. Maddie, like so many, couldn't wait for her first chapter to begin. Raven, however, was less hexcited.

Raven had been dreading this year. She didn't want to be the Evil Queen. But what choice did she have? As Headmaster Grimm always said, the students had to follow their fairytale destinies. Everyone always signed the Storybook of Legends on Legacy Day. And that meant Raven would have to as well.

During orientation, everyone split into story groups for their yearly tour. While Maddie skipped happily to Professor Rumpelstiltskin's group of quirky characters, Raven was grouped with the other "villains."

The scary, hairy Professor Badwolf snarled, "You will follow me." He took them down to the dark cauldron room, where they would learn the toil and trouble of potion making. Raven didn't like the idea of causing trouble one bit.

After the tour, Raven returned to the dorms, feeling flustered. She wasn't a villain—not at heart, anyway. She wondered what her life might be like if she weren't the future Evil Queen, but just Raven. She knew she was supposed to follow in her mother's evil footsteps, but she truthfully never wanted to be a bad guy. She always wanted to make the world happier.

When Raven was a little girl, she would cast spells that made flowers burst into butterflies! Then one day, her magic just didn't work right, and instead the flowers burst into flames. Ever since then, her magic backfired whenever she used it for good. When she tried to help others, it ended up making things worse. Raven thought she would get in trouble for accidentally casting evil spells, but it only made her mother prouder.

Raven finally fell asleep, wishing that there were some way to change her destiny.

The next day, Raven went to visit her advisor, Madam Baba Yaga, to go over her class schedule. Raven was supposed to take General Villainy, Home Evilnomics, Magicology, History of Evil Spells, and Witchness Management. They were all villain classes!

"Don't I have any choice in what classes I want to take?" Raven asked without thinking. The words just slipped out.

Madam Baba Yaga looked hard at Raven for a long while. "You know perfectly well it is school policy to take the classes best suited for your destiny," she said, finally breaking her stare. "However, you may choose one class of your own, Ms. Queen."

Raven didn't need to think twice. She wanted to take Muse-ic Class. It was traditionally a class for princesses only, but singing always set her free.

Madam Baba Yaga thought for another long moment.

"I will inform Professor Pied Piper immediately. I expect no more talk of choice. Are we clear?" she said sternly. Raven nodded. "Now go to the library to receive your hextbooks."

Raven arrived at the library and found Maddie, bouncing around hexstatically. She was going on and on about something that Raven needed to see, but nobody could find. Sometimes Maddie spoke in a silly Wonderlandian language called Riddlish. It always sounded like nonsense to Raven. When Maddie couldn't explain what she wanted to say, she grabbed Raven's hand and guided her through the library to a secret door she'd found.

Maddie knocked a playful rhythm, and in a flash, they were suddenly surrounded by a ring of ancient, dusty books.

"Maddie, where are we?" Raven asked.

Maddie explained they were in the Vault of Lost Tales, where the Master Librarian, Giles Grimm, lived. She told Raven that he had something important to tell her.

When they found Giles Grimm, he was buried under piles of books. His eyes darted back and forth across the pages of a large tome. He started speaking, and Raven realized he was speaking in Riddlish. He'd been cursed by a babbling spell, and only Maddie could understand him.

After they spoke, Maddie told Raven something that would change her friend forever: According to the Master Librarian, if Raven pledged to create her own Happily Ever After, she would be free to write her own story.

Could it be true? Raven had spent her entire life thinking she had to be the Evil Queen. She and her classmates had been told to follow their destinies, no matter what. Did Raven dare to be just Raven instead? If she flipped the script, what would happen? And what would people think?

But then, Raven thought, maybe there were others who wanted a chance to write their own Happily Ever After, too. And it was up to Raven to give them the chance. So that Legacy Day, Raven would rewrite her script.

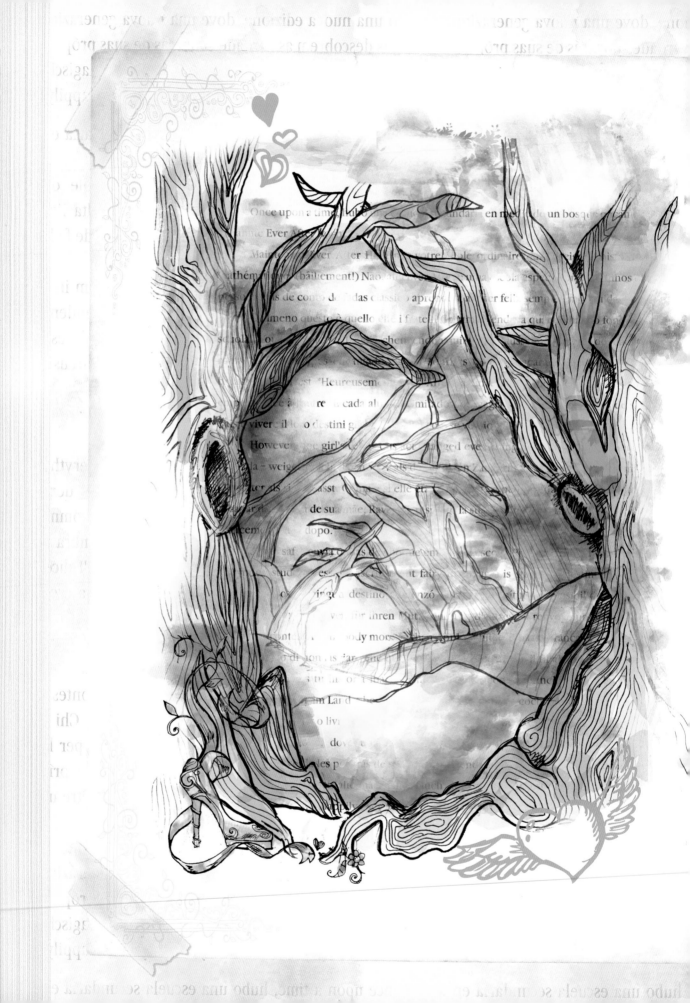

Ashlynn Ella

Ever since Ashlynn Ella was little, she had been told that everyone at Ever After High wished they had her Happily Ever After. She was Cinderella's daughter, and one day, when the shoe fit, she'd be swept away by her Prince Charming. Still, Ashlynn never wanted to be swept away by some prince. Instead, she thought true love should happen naturally, not by the storybook. But could Ashlynn have a fairytale romance that was never meant to be? She was so royally torn.

So on the fairy first day of Damsel-In-Distressing class, Ashlynn wasn't hexcited when their teacher announced that she would be paired with Daring Charming. Daring wasn't fairy princely, and he wasn't even supposed to be Ashlynn's prince! She let out a big groan. It was going to be a long school year.

After class was finished, Ashlynn needed to clear her head. So she went to the most calming place she knew: the Enchanted Forest. The Enchanted Forest was where magic blossomed and oh-so-cute-and-cuddly woodland creatures lived and played.

Every fairytale
princess had a special
connection to the woodland
creatures, but only Ashlynn could
actually understand what they were
saying. Sometimes the animals made
more sense to her than people.

Ashlynn breathed in the
spellbinding scent of the
charm blossom petals. She
closed her eyes and enjoyed
the sounds of birds chirping
and leaves rustling. Then
suddenly, an animal
shouted, "Help!"
Ashlynn jumped
into action.

Branches lifted themselves out of Ashlynn's way as she hurried through the clearing. When she found the animal, she could hardly believe her eyes! There was a helpless squirrel stuck to a tree, and Hunter Huntsman was lifting his axe.

"No!" she shouted as she ran toward Hunter. With all her strength, Ashlynn pushed him face-first into the mud. She couldn't let him hurt that poor squirrel.

"Hey, what's the big idea?" the squirrel chittered. An arrow pinned him to the tree by the satchel around his little squirrel waist.

Ashlynn scratched her head. "I just saved you from the scary huntsman!" she said.

"Hunter? Scary?" the squirrel replied, bursting with laughter. "He's my friend!"

"Pesky!" Hunter called out to his pet squirrel as he lifted himself up from the mud.

Before Ashlynn could blink, Hunter plucked the arrow from the tree and caught Pesky in his hand. He bandaged Pesky from head to tail.

Hunter had been trying to save the squirrel, not hurt him. Ashlynn was so embarrassed. "Sorry I pushed you," she said.

He turned, and their eyes met for the first time. Time stood still. His hazel eyes were gentle and warm. Her heart thumped in her throat. Was she sick? Her feet felt really weird in her heels.

Hunter offered to walk Ashlynn back to school. On their walk, Ashlynn was surprised by how much they had in common. They both loved nature and caring for animals. She was totally throne for a loop! Hunter wasn't some big ogre. He was totally charming!

Ashlynn could've talked to Hunter forever after, but soon enough they were inside the school's castle. She was twirling her hair, not wanting to say good-bye, when she realized her ring was missing. "Oh no!" she cried. "My family ring! It must have fallen off in the forest!"

Hunter's face lit up. "Maybe we could go back to the forest and search for it," Hunter said nervously before adding, "And maybe we could have a picnic, too."

Ashlynn's heart raced. "Hunter, I'd love to go on a picnic with you."

His eyes widened. "Really? I mean…cool," he said, trying not to show how hexcited he was. He paused for a moment, then finally said, "Hext you later." Then Hunter raced off in the other direction.

Ashlynn couldn't believe it! The day totally flipped the script! She'd gone into the forest worried about one fairytale prince, but she exited having her fairytale dream come true. Ashlynn spun around and skipped all the way to her dorm.

But when Ashlynn was back in her room, she realized that she and Hunter couldn't have a Happily Ever After. He wasn't her fairytale prince. Ashlynn had never been so upset.

The next day, Ashlynn went to the Enchanted Forest at sunset to clear her head. The sun hung low in the sky. The air was still and crisp. The trees looked lonely, save for branches reaching toward one another. The seconds passed like hours. Finally, Ashlynn heard a rustling coming from the trees, and Hunter walked into sight, looking adorably silly. He wore a prince's jacket that was way too small for him, and he carried a giant bouquet of charm blossoms. Hunter bent to kiss her hand and his jacket ripped!

She lifted his face and let out a laugh. "Oh, Hunter, what are you wearing?" she asked.

"I borrowed one of Dexter's old jackets and ties," he wheezed. "Every princess needs a prince."

Ashlynn laughed again. "You don't need to be a prince for me!" she said.

Hunter took her hand, and it felt like a bolt of lightning ran up her arm. "I found your ring," he said as he pulled Ashlynn's family ring from his pocket. Ashlynn's heart raced again. The world brightened. Her true hero saved the day! As she threw her arms around him, something still bothered her. "Hunter, if anyone finds out—" she began.

He gave her a smile that Ashlynn would cherish forever after. "It will just have to stay our little secret." He gave her a big, warm hug—and the stars started sparkling again.

Holly O'Hair

After years spent memorizing every fairytale, writing about her favorite legends, and, of course, studying her own fairytale, Holly O'Hair was finally going to let her hair down at Ever After High! This was her first time living outside the tower. She was hair over heels with hexcitement! She was the daughter of Rapunzel, ever after all.

Actually, she wasn't the only daughter of Rapunzel. She had an identical twin, Poppy, who couldn't go to Ever After High. Holly was born just a hair before her sister, making the family legacy her responsibility. Poppy was destined to be a fairytale without a story, and Holly knew it always secretly bothered her sister. So Holly promised herself she would make sure Poppy could join her at Ever After High. The night before Holly left for school, she looked at the stars outside the tower window and wished that both of them could have a Once Upon a Time.

Ever After High was like all Holly's favorite storybooks coming to life to hang out together. But she was most excited about Legacy Day. That was when the new generation of fairytales signed the Storybook of Legends to bind themselves to their destinies. Holly couldn't wait to declare her destiny as the next Rapunzel!

That year, however, the script was flipped. Raven Queen declared she wasn't going to be the next Evil Queen. She was going to rewrite her own Happily Ever After. Did Raven's actions mean that destiny wasn't set in stone?

Then Holly realized this might be her wish come true. If destiny wasn't a sure thing, maybe the O'Hair twins could actually be at Ever After High together! Holly could be the next Rapunzel, and Poppy could write her own story.

Holly ran to Headmaster Grimm and asked him if Poppy could come to Ever After High, since Raven had proved she didn't need to have a prewritten story.

Headmaster Grimm slowly turned. His face was redder than a riding hood. "Ms. O'Hair," he growled through clenched teeth, "your sister can *never* come to Ever After High! Not while I'm headmaster!"

But Holly was positive there had to be a way to change his mind.

Holly went to visit her sister in the Tower Hair Salon where Poppy was attending beauty school to become the most fableous stylist ever after. Ever since they were kids, Poppy always loved styling hair. In fact, she styled her own hair in a new way every morning. Now her schedule was always royally booked! But she always made time for Holly.

When Holly rushed into the salon, she just couldn't wait to tell Poppy the big news! "Raven Queen declared to not follow her destiny! Maybe that means you can write your own Happily Ever After!" Holly said hexcitedly.

Poppy wasn't so sure. It was one thing to refuse to follow your storybook destiny. It was another to not have a destiny at all. But Holly

pleaded with Poppy to consider attending Ever After High if she could convince Headmaster Grimm to allow it.

Poppy laughed. "If you can change his mind, not only will I go to Ever After High, but you can borrow any of my scarves for a month," she said.

It was a win-win, and Holly pinkie-promised to seal the deal!

Now that Poppy had agreed to come to Ever After High, Holly just had to find a way to make it happen. Over the next several days, Holly sat in the library and reread every story that she knew, searching for new meanings about finding your own destiny. But every story seemed hexactly the same as the last time she read it.

Then Holly suddenly heard a knocking. She looked around the library to find the source, but nothing was out of the ordinary. Then she heard the knocking again. It wasn't coming from a door. No, the knocking was coming from under the floor!

Holly followed the sound until it stopped suddenly and an old book fell in front of her. She wiped the dust from its cover and read: *The Origin of Ever After High* by M. Grimm & G. Grimm. The headmaster must have written this book with his brother! Then, curiously, the book opened on its own. Holly read the page before her and gasped joyfully. If this book wasn't going to convince Headmaster Grimm to let Poppy join Ever After High, nothing would.

Holly took the book and went straight to the headmaster's office. Upon entering, she placed

The Origin of Ever After High on his desk and showed him the page that had opened magically. It said Ever After High welcomed all the children of fairytale legends to learn the art of fulfilling their destinies.

He looked at Holly hexpectantly.

"*All* the children of fairytale legends, sir. My sister should be allowed to come to Ever After High. You wrote the rule yourself, Headmaster," Holly explained.

Headmaster Grimm considered this for a moment and sighed. "Very well, Ms. O'Hair," he said. "Your sister may attend Ever After High."

"Thank you, sir!" Holly said happily. She ran straight for the Tower Salon to tell Poppy the great news!

On Poppy's first day at school, everyone asked Holly if she ever doubted that Poppy would come to Ever After High. Of course she didn't! It was destined to come true.

Cedar Wood

After Cedar Wood, the daughter of Pinocchio, was carved from magical wood, her father wished for the Blue-Haired Fairy to make her kind, caring, and honest. But Cedar wished he'd spent a little more time thinking about his word choice. The Fairy took him way too literally. Now she had to tell the truth no matter what.

So how was Cedar supposed to become a real girl? The entire Pinocchio story was about searching her heart for the right choices. And Cedar didn't *have* any choice!

Art was Cedar Wood's favorite class. Truthfully,

it was her only real outlet. She could plug in her headphones, turn up her muse-ic, dip her brush, and paint away. She never had to worry about truth or lies, curses or wishes. There was something about a blank canvas that felt…free.

But Cedar was throne
for a loop by her latest
assignment: joy. The class had
to paint something that was full
of joy, but that seemed impossible
to Cedar. How could she paint a
feeling? All she felt was confused.
Cedar finally decided to paint the
moment when she would become
a real girl. It seemed like a happy
moment, right?

As she finished, Professor Card came over to her easel. He tapped his chin thoughtfully. "Technically, it's perfect. Yet emotionally, it's empty. I can tell you want me to feel happiness, but I don't feel your joy. Real joy," he said.

Cedar's heart went timber.

"How do you paint 'joy,' sir?" she asked.

"Cedar"—Professor Card smiled kindly—"find your true voice. Then you'll know."

Cedar left class more confused than ever after before. "How do I find my true voice?" she asked herself. She knew what it was like to tell the truth. In fact, she could only ever tell the truth. But Cedar's painting was of something that hadn't really happened yet. *Maybe that's why the painting didn't feel like real joy*, she thought. So Cedar needed a way to find the truth. She was getting a splintering headache just thinking about it!

Cedar went to the Mad Hatter of Wonderland's Haberdashery & Tea Shoppe for a hot cup of willow sap tea to make her feel better. There she found...Madeline Hatter! Maddie hopped onto a chair next to Cedar.

"It looks like you could use a friend," she said.

Cedar told Maddie that she couldn't find her voice.

"So where do you think you left your voice?" Maddie asked. When Cedar explained that she was trying to find her voice in Arts & Crafts, Maddie got confused. "You don't use your voice in art. You use paint. That's a riddle fiddle." Then Maddie's eyes lit up! "Voice…paint… riddle! I've got it!"

Maddie grabbed a heart-shaped key, and unlocked a heart-shaped door in the corner of the Tea Shoppe. On the other side of the door, they found Lizzie Hearts playing Wonderland croquet. Lizzie was the daughter of the Queen of Hearts and the heir to Wonderland's throne.

"If anyone can help you, she can," Maddie whispered.

Maddie told Lizzie all about how Cedar
needed to find her voice.

Lizzie thought about it for a moment before
speaking. "Paint the roses!" she demanded,
pointing to a white rose bush with a can of red
paint next to it.

Cedar's eyes darted to Maddie, who smiled
and nodded. Cedar dipped the brush into the
paint. As soon as her brush touched the petal,
Lizzie snatched the brush from Cedar's hand.
"Off with her head! Paint the roses red!" she
shouted.

Lizzie handed back the brush. Cedar asked Maddie to help her understand. "What does she want?"

"She wants you to paint the roses red. Or she doesn't. Maybe the rose knows," Maddie replied with a shrug.

So, feeling a bit silly, Cedar leaned over to ask
the rose bush what Lizzie wanted. Of course, it
didn't answer. Yet Lizzie nodded. Cedar asked
herself over and over again, "How do I paint
the roses red without painting the roses red?"

After what felt like forever after, something novel happened. A gentle breeze blew. The rose gracefully fluttered in the wind. The sun's rays kissed its petals, making them turn from snow white to sunset red. It was simply the most beautiful thing in the world.

Cedar smiled at Lizzie. Ever so slightly, Lizzie smiled back. The roses had been painted red with a little patience.

By the time Cedar had her next Arts & Crafts class, she was confident that she knew her own voice. She closed her eyes and remembered how special it made her feel, knowing she had to be at that exact spot in that exact moment to see a simple rose brighten the world. First she sketched, then dipped her brush in her watercolors and started painting a sunset-red rose.

Professor Card grinned from ear to ear,
"Spelltacular!" he said. "I feel joy in every
brushstroke. How did you find your voice?"

Cedar put down her brush to admire her painting. "Even though I'm not a real girl yet, I do have real feelings," she said. "I don't need to overthink happiness. Sometimes it's as simple as stopping to smell the roses. And that's no lie!"

Madeline Hatter—or Maddie for short—couldn't wait to follow in her father's footsteps to become the next Mad Hatter. She loved throwing tea parties and solving riddles, just like they did at home in Wonderland. This year, everyone would take their first step toward their fairytale futures. It was Legacy Year, and all the students had to pledge to follow their fairytale destinies.

Maddie was excited to be the next Mad Hatter, but Raven Queen, Maddie's best friend forever after, wasn't so lucky. Her mom was the wicked Evil Queen from Snow White's story, and Raven was just wicked awesome. Raven wanted nothing more than to leave the poison apples to the real villains and make people happy!

During their first week at school, Raven and Maddie had been separated into two groups: Raven had to go with the villains, and Maddie went with all the other silly fairytales. Maddie was trailing behind her group, jumping around backward with one foot in the air. She jumped all the way until she bumped into Kitty Cheshire, her old friend from Wonderland. Kitty was the daughter of the Cheshire Cat, and she was always ready with a riddle for Maddie.

Seeing Maddie, Kitty perked up and scribbled something on a piece of paper. "I have a riddle for you," she said as she gave Maddie the doodle she'd just made. Maddie examined the drawing. It was of a monster smashing a town.

"What's this worth to you?" Kitty asked mischievously.

"Oh, Kitty! That's too easy," answered Maddie. She could solve the first clue to Kitty's riddle. She had drawn her a picture, and a picture was worth a thousand words. That meant that Maddie had to look for the answer to Kitty's riddle in the best place to find words: the library!

Maddie dashed away to find the answer as Kitty roared with laughter. Maddie would show her! She couldn't be out-riddled!

Maddie loved when the unhexpected happened! Just like when she hexpected the step-librarian to help, but all she did was shush her. So Maddie read through the *Encyclopedia of Monsters* and *History of Villages & the Beasts that Destroyed Them* before realizing they were more frightening than helpful.

Right when Maddie was going to give up, she heard a knocking coming from the distance. There was something familiar about it. It wasn't a knock that said, "Hello, I'm at the door." No, it was more like, "Find me if you can." Maddie loved to play hide-and-go-seek! She also loved knock-knock jokes. The mysterious knocking was like two goodies wrapped into one! She knocked back: "Ready or not, here I come!"

She followed the knocking deep into the library. *This must be how Hansel and Gretel felt following the breadcrumbs!* she thought.

Maddie followed the knocking all the way to the back of the library, where she hit a wall. But it was a secret-door wall! Maddie knocked and said, "I found you. Now let me in."

With a flash, Maddie was transported from
the school library to a maze filled with dusty,
old books. The knocking was much louder in
there. Maddie twisted, wound, and rounded
through the hallways until finally she walked into
an office with books scattered all over. Sitting
at a desk was an old, bearded man knocking
on its surface. And imagine her surprise when
he spoke to her in Riddlish! Riddlish was the
language everyone in Wonderland spoke.

"Tapping two ways trickle down, unto too trickle upside frown!" he said upon seeing Maddie enter the room. Maddie understood that he meant "I'm so happy! Someone finally heard my knocking call!"

She grinned and responded in Riddlish, too. "White knight, sunshine; a place, a face, I have mine?" That meant "Hello, what's your name?"

The old man realized that Maddie must be the daughter of the Mad Hatter. He introduced himself as Giles Grimm, the Master Librarian.

Librarian Grimm was cursed by a babbling spell and locked in the Vault of Lost Tales. Now he spent his days searching for the spell to break the curse. Then it dawned on Maddie: Raven knew about spells! Maddie told him, but he looked worried. Even though Raven was the daughter of the Evil Queen, sometimes her spells didn't always go as planned. Whenever she used her magic for good, the spells would backfire. Maddie could tell he was also worried that Raven might be mean, just because of who her mom was.

"She's really nice," Maddie reassured him, "She doesn't even want to be the Evil Queen."

Suddenly, Librarian Grimm shot out of his chair and said that Maddie must bring Raven to him. He had something to tell her.

Maddie searched all over for Raven. Finally, when there was nowhere else to look, she went back to the library, and there Raven was! What luck! Maddie tried to tell her what happened, but Raven couldn't understand. Maybe Maddie was still speaking Riddlish. So she just took her to the Vault of Lost Tales.

When Maddie brought Raven to Librarian
Grimm, he slammed the book he was reading.
"Flipping flapjacks, ripping rust! Cutting
corners dawn to dust!" he said
loudly. Maddie hexplained
that he was saying he was
frustrated by how long it
was taking to find the spell
he needed.

Maddie approached him. "Horseshoes, clovers, rabbits feet! Feathers, friends, we share a seat!" That meant "Luckily for you, Raven and I are here to help."

The next bit of Riddlish was a jumble. But when he pointed at Raven, Maddie was pretty sure he meant "Listen, daughter of the Evil Queen. Destiny is a myth. If you pledge on Legacy Day to rewrite your own destiny, everyone will be free to choose their own Happily Ever After!"

The Master Librarian thought it was more important that Raven follow her heart. Maybe then they could lift his babbling curse. But for now, Raven could go and write her own story.

Tea-rrific! thought Maddie. It was everything Raven always wanted! She didn't have to be the Evil Queen! Nobody had to follow their parents' stories! Not even Maddie!

Wait a spell…thought Maddie. She didn't have to follow her destiny? She loved that she would get to be the next Mad Hatter. The tea parties, the riddle games, the fun with talking bunnies— those were all her favorite things! But Maddie could worry about that later. Raven finally had hope. And right now, she needed a Happily Ever After.

Melody Piper

Melody Piper and her dad, the Pied Piper, were just the same—they both loved muse-ic and their legacies. And after she finished at Ever After High, Melody would follow in her dad's footsteps. Just like her dad, she believed that muse-ic should enchant people to come together and dance. Melody thought that must be why they had such a great father-daughter relationship. He accepted her for who she was. With his encouragement, Melody listened to her heart to become Ever After High's most inspiring DJ!

One night, Melody was creating a new remix when Briar Beauty hext messaged her. Briar wasn't just the daughter of Sleeping Beauty; she was also the social throne of the Royal Student Council. She was responsible for making sure every party at school was legendary.

Briar wanted Melody to DJ Holly and Poppy O'Hair's birthday bash. Melody couldn't wait to create an awesome set for Rapunzel twins' party. There was only one catch….

Holly and Poppy might have looked identical, but their muse-ical tastes were royally different. Holly liked slow, romantic ballads, while Poppy liked loud, banging rock. Mixing the two styles of muse-ic was going to be wicked hard, but Melody was determined to get it right.

Over the next couple of days, Melody created a ton of different remixes combining the two different types of muse-ic. But days turned into weeks, and she still couldn't get a full set together. The two styles were just too different. Still, she wasn't about to give up!

But the more time Melody spent on the remix, the more it sounded like a carriagewreck.

"What's that noise?" Ginger Breadhouse shouted as she walked into the room. Ginger was the daughter of the Candy Witch from Hansel and Gretel, but she wasn't a villain at heart. Really, she just wanted to cook. She was also Melody's roommate and great friend. Her pots and pans scattered all over the floor as she raced over and shut down Melody's muse-ic app. "Is that the birthday remix? It's, um…really…" Ginger's voice trailed off.

Melody sighed. "I know, I know. It's a total fairy-fail," she said.

Ginger patted her on the back. "Oh, Melody, why didn't you ask for help? We're all friends," she asked.

Melody was ashamed. "What am I going to do? I want to help make Holly and Poppy's birthday legendary, but none of my mixes are working."

"*Hmmm.*" Ginger pulled a green carrot and a handful of purple beans from her bookpack. "This is Bitter Witches Root. And these are Troll Slime Beans."

"Gross!" Melody tightened her mouth.

"Totally." Ginger reached back into her bookpack. "But when you crumble in some honeycomb and add a dash of mint, something amazing happens." Ginger handed Melody a cupcake. Surprisingly, it was sweet and refreshing. "Instead of just trying to mix two things that don't go together, maybe look for your secret ingredient." Ginger was right, and Melody knew hexactly where to go.

Muse-ic Class was one of the most popular classes at Ever After High. It was where people came to sing their true hearts out, or band together with magical instruments. Plus, it was taught by Melody's dad.

As Melody walked down the hallway, she heard the most spellbinding singing voice. It was coming from the Muse-ic room. She opened the door, and there, all alone, was someone she'd never met before. She had coral-colored hair and a sea-foam dress. She clammed up as soon as Melody saw her.

"Sorry," she said as she quickly scuttled away.

"Wait!" Melody called, and the girl stopped in her tracks. "I didn't mean to scare you. My name's Melody. I'm the Pied Piper's daughter." She extended her hand.

The girl looked at it for a moment, and then shook it. "I am Meeshell Mermaid, the next Little Mermaid."

Melody grinned. "Well, Meeshell, your singing voice is once upon amazing!" she said. "I'm into muse-ic, too."

They talked about their favorite types of muse-ic. They shared songs from their MirrorPhones. Before long, Melody told her all about her birthday remix problem and what she was looking for.

"*Hmmm…*" Meeshell sang as she tapped her chin rhythmically. "What do you suppose this missing ingredient could be?"

Then the answer popped into Melody's head. All she needed was Meeshell's help.

Immediately, the set list came together. Bursting with creativity, Melody crammed weeks of work into just a few days. At the last minute, she finally finished the mix. Melody quickly packed her DJ bag and rushed to the Tower Hair Salon, where the twins would have their party.

Briar ran toward her. "Thank fairy godmother!" she said. "For a minute I was afraid you weren't going to show."

Melody leaped behind the DJ table. "You know I wouldn't miss it for the world," she said. Melody plugged in her headphones and turned on her mixing board, and one-by-one, people started showing up. Less than an hour later, the place was packed.

When Holly and Poppy arrived, they screamed with joy. "This is happily ever awesome!" they said in unison.

Briar led the crowd in singing "Fairest Birthday" to Holly and Poppy. "And now," Briar

continued, "your favorite DJ and mine…Melody Piper!"

Melody started the song. A slow beat rose, and Meeshell started singing. She was fableous enough to let Melody record her voice, and it was just the secret ingredient Melody had been looking for. It connected the two beats perfectly!

Pretty soon, everyone was dancing. Poppy started jumping as Holly swayed smoothly back and forth.

Everyone danced until they couldn't dance anymore. It was legendary! Holly and Poppy thanked Melody for playing the most memorable birthday soundtrack ever after.

At the end of the night, as she packed up her DJ gear, Melody felt a tap on her shoulder.

It was Ginger and Meeshell, and she felt like the luckiest DJ in the world. Not because she'd played a great mix, but because it seemed no matter where she turned, she could count on friends both old and new to help her out of a jam.

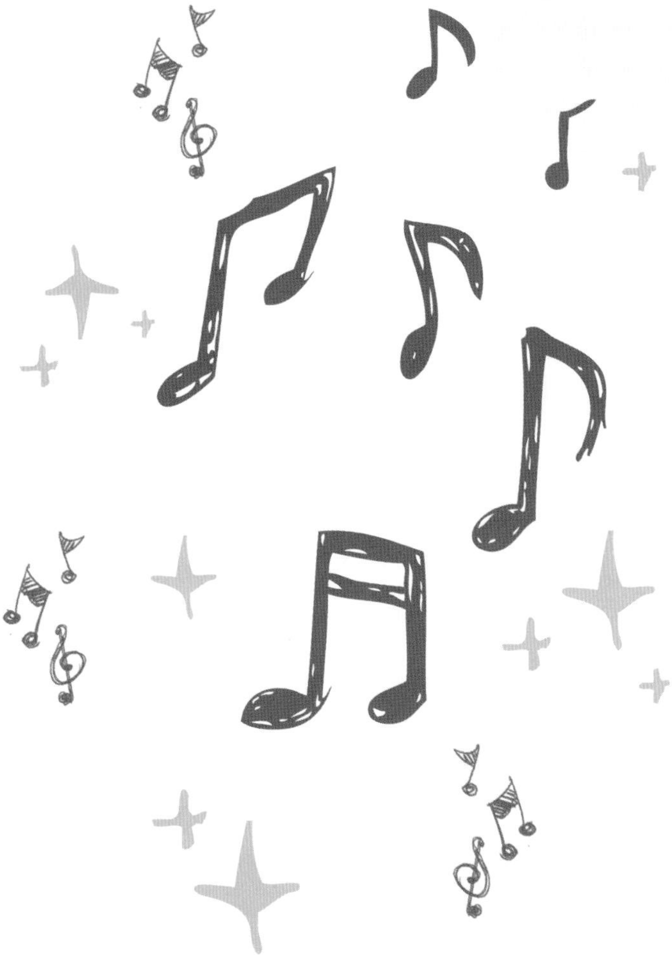

Apple White

Life can be wonderful when you have a Happily Ever After. Take Apple White for example. Since her mother was the royally famous Snow White, it was her destiny to follow in her footsteps. It was a fableous future filled with friendly dwarves, her fairy own Prince Charming, and a magical wedding that ended with a big musical number, with everyone in the kingdom knowing all the words! Still… Apple never took her prewritten legacy for granted. That was why she studied hard at Ever After High.

There was a lot of pressure for Apple as the next in line to be "the Fairest of Them All." But it was worth the work.

Once upon a new school year, one week before classes, the students of Ever After High had their "Book-to-School" orientation in the Charmitorium. Apple White was looking forward to Headmaster Grimm's welcome-back speech. He always reminded the students of how they were all destined for greatness. There was no such thing as short stories or small tales. They were all pages in the big book of life, and they all had roles to play.

And this year was fairy important because it was the year all the fairytales would finally sign the Storybook of Legends. Apple had dreamed of this year since she was in nursery-rhyme school. On Legacy Day, she would unlock the Storybook of Legends and declare her destiny. She couldn't wait to start the path to her first chapter as Snow White!

That was, until Raven Queen started to question her own fate. As the daughter of the Evil Queen, Raven was destined to become the Evil Queen in Snow White's story. But Raven wasn't so sure she wanted to be a villain. Everyone was worried that if Raven did not follow her destiny, the whole storybook would fall apart!

Apple didn't understand why Raven was questioning her story. What was wrong with the way things were once upon a time? Apple wondered. Whatever your parent's role was, that was your role, too. If your mom was the Evil Queen, it was your job to be the next Evil Queen. It was written that way for a reason!

Briar Beauty saw Apple worrying about Legacy Day and invited her to go on a shopping trip. Just over the bridge from school was the best shopping in the land—the Village Mall in the Village of Book End. Apple and Briar knew they shouldn't leave school in the middle of orientation, but they both thought a quick trip couldn't hurt anyone.

They shopped around for a bit, stopping in the Tower Hair Salon and the MirrorPad store. But before long there was a wicked surprise waiting for Apple and Briar around the next corner. Madam Baba Yaga, the school's advisor for sorceresses, had heard they were skipping orientation.

"I trust you have a note hexcusing you from orientation?" she said.

Apple had broken a rule, and she knew she was in trouble. Madam Baba Yaga clapped her hands twice, and in a sudden *puff*, Apple was in detention.

The year was starting off on the wrong slipper. Apple was mad at herself. Her parents had invested so much in her future. But now she was in detention, waiting to see Headmaster Grimm. Apple was disappointed she hadn't set a better hexample. If she was supposed to be the future queen, she needed to act like it. Otherwise they might close the book on her.

See, if a character rebelled against the system, their story would be forever locked, and they would vanish from memory. So being the next Snow White was not just about being beautiful and popular. If Apple was lucky enough to get out of this mess, she was going to be the best Fairest One of All the school had ever after seen. And that was just what Apple was going to tell Headmaster Grimm.

As if on cue, a door opened, and imagine Apple's surprise when Briar poked her head in and said, "The headmaster wants to see you."

Usually Apple didn't consider it charming to cry in public. But in the case of being sent to the headmaster's office, she'd make a hexception. Apple broke down in tears, but the headmaster was kind as always. He calmed her down, and hexplained that while he was shocked Apple had broken the rules, he understood what it was like to be young.

But Apple still felt terrible about breaking the rules and setting a bad hexample. She wanted to do something good to make it up to everyone. Apple asked if there was anything she could do to make it better.

The headmaster smiled. "There is one thing," he said. "It has come to my attention that Raven Queen may be unhappy with her destiny. As the Evil Queen, it is important that she embraces her legacy. Can you think of anything to help?"

Apple knew that Raven had been questioning her destiny, but she never imagined that Raven might not sign the Storybook of Legends. And if she didn't, Raven was in danger of vanishing from memory!

Apple knew what she had to do. "Sir, I formally request a transfer to room with Raven Queen," she said confidently.

And so Apple and Raven became roommates, and soon they'd be friends. Some people might have thought it odd for a princess to be friends with an evil sorceress, but if Apple could help Raven see the light, it would all be worth it. But that was a story for another day.

Lizzie Hearts

Lizzie Hearts royally loved Wonderland. It was simply the most nonsensical, riddle-tastic, wonderlandiful place ever after. It was also her home. And she missed it dearly. As the daughter of the Queen of Hearts, it was her destiny to rule Wonderland one day. Instead, Lizzie was at Ever After High, where she didn't feel like she fit in. People seemed to believe Lizzie was a few cards short of a full deck because she often yelled, "Off with your head!" But where she came from, that phrase was simply a common courtesy.

If someone brought tea, it was polite to thank him or her by saying, "Off with your head!" But her new classmates took Lizzie fairy literally.

Lizzie didn't understand Ever After High. She thought everyone saw things in black and red. But she was trying to fit in, because Lizzie feared she may never see Wonderland again.

Lizzie was grateful to still have some of her Wonderlandian friends in Ever After, too. The White Queen, who co-rules Wonderland with Lizzie's mom, had also come to Ever After High. She was now Lizzie's Princessology teacher, and as such, Lizzie respectfully referred to her as "Mrs. Her Majesty the White Queen." However, when the White Queen said Lizzie had to meet her after class, Lizzie was quite upset.

"Am I in trouble again?" Lizzie asked.

"You are not in trouble," Mrs. Her Majesty the White Queen said delicately. "However, I've noticed you've had trouble making new friends. Perhaps you should stop shouting 'Off with your head' so much. Your classmates take it quite literally."

"What a bunch of Alices," Lizzie mumbled under her breath. She was upset because no one at Ever After High seemed to understand her. She wished with all her heart that she could be in Wonderland again.

"Lizzie, this is home now," Mrs. Her Majesty the White Queen reminded her.

"Home? I have no home," Lizzie said as she slammed the door behind her as hard as she could.

Even though it was Lizzie's destiny to be angry, she was usually quite calm. In fact, ever since she was three-of-hearts old, she spent hours working on her non-anger management. It was difficult at times, but her mother was always supportive. She wanted Lizzie to have the best childhood ever after.

Then one day, the Evil Queen came to Wonderland and destroyed everything. Lizzie was locked away in her bedroom when she heard the familiar POOF! of a Cheshire Cat appearing from thin air. It was Lizzie's best friend forever after, Kitty Cheshire, and she had never been happier to see her.

With tears in her eyes, Kitty hugged
Lizzie and told her they would have to leave
Wonderland. They ran out of the castle, and
traveled up the rabbit hole into the land of Ever
After. The rabbit hole was then sealed, and a
wishing well was built over it. That was the last
time Lizzie saw Wonderland.

Every day Lizzie would visit the wishing well and wish with all her heart to go home. One day, as Lizzie was sitting by the well, Kitty appeared. Lizzie shared how much she wanted to go home, but she knew the rabbit hole wouldn't reopen.

"This is all just part of the story," Kitty said.

"Not my story," Lizzie replied as she sat next to Kitty. "I can't be myself here. Everyone thinks I'm mad."

"Lizzie, we're all mad," Kitty said, laughing. "We're from Wonderland after all. Madness makes us special, especially here."

But nothing Kitty could say would make Lizzie feel better.

Then Kitty's wide Cheshire grin spread across her face. "I know just what you need to feel better."

In an instant, they appeared on the school's playing field. Kitty vanished, then reappeared carrying a large sack. "Since you miss home so much, we should bring a little bit of home here," Kitty said. She turned the sack upside down, and out came flamingos and hedgehogs! To Lizzie, that could only mean one thing: Wonderland croquet!

As they set up the field, Madeline Hatter walked over to them with Cedar Wood, the daughter of Pinocchio. Maddie was chipper as ever. "Crowns and kettles, together again," she said in Riddlish, greeting her fellow Wonderlandians.

Maddie told Lizzie that she was helping Cedar find her voice as an artist. Lizzie's eyes lit up. She realized this was her chance to help someone who was lost, just like Alice was in Wonderland. For a brief moment, Cedar was her new Alice.

Lizzie presented Cedar with a riddle. "Paint the roses red," she said, meaning that Cedar should take time to search her heart for what truly inspired her. When Cedar finally figured out the riddle, they shared a smile. Cedar found her answer, and Lizzie did, too. It just took her a while to realize it.

Lizzie went straight to the White Queen's office to apologize for how she had behaved that morning. "I'm sorry, Mrs. Your Majesty the White Queen," she said. "I was angry, but that's no hexcuse for losing my manners. Ever since we fled our home, I've been so focused on my sadness, when I should be helping others like the future Queen of Hearts Wonderlandians need."

Slowly, Mrs. Her Majesty the White Queen smiled and invited Lizzie to talk about what was making her sad.

Lizzie explained that she hadn't felt much like herself, but she had finally figured out why.

She'd felt fairy far away from home ever since the rabbit hole was sealed. She and all the Wonderlandians were cut off from the unique magic that made them special.

Lizzie and Mrs. Her Majesty the White Queen

came up with a plan to help the Wonderlandians feel more connected to their home. They would build a special place filled with Wonderland enchantments, right by the wishing well, and call it Wonderland Grove.

Lizzie felt like her old self again. Just because she couldn't go back to Wonderland didn't mean she couldn't make Ever After High her new home. Ever after all, the Queen of Hearts is the heart of Wonderland. And home is always where the heart is.

Ginger Breadhouse

Before Ginger Breadhouse's first day at Ever After High, her mom—the Candy Witch from Hansel and Gretel—told her the secret ingredient for making it through school: the eviler, the better. But Ginger didn't like that idea. She was tired of people following breadcrumbs to her gingerbread cabin in the Dark Forest, only to run away screaming, "Witch, witch!"

Ginger thought good food should bring people together. That's all she ever wanted to do. So when it came time to complete her midterm hexam, in which Ginger was supposed to trap Helga and Gus Crumb—the next Hansel and Gretel—and prepare them for a witch's stew, she instead prepared a five-course dinner and thanked them for coming after they ate their fill. That change did not go over well with her teacher Madam Yaga or Headmaster Grimm.

Ginger was called to Madam Baba Yaga's office to discuss her hexam performance. Madam Baba Yaga sat behind her desk next to a scowling Helga and her hysterically sobbing cousin, Gus.

Helga pointed an accusing finger at Ginger. "You vere supposed to put Gus in de cage!" she said.

"All I vanted vas to eat candy!" Gus added between sobs. "Now ve flunked and it's all your fault!"

Ginger's heart raced. Why hadn't she just done what she was told? She felt like she'd let everyone down.

Madam Baba Yaga grinned toothily. "Oh, nobody failed. Helga and Gus have passed because they tried to do their part," she explained to Ginger's relief. "But, Ginger, we're only going to give you one more chance. This time, I'll play Gretel, and the headmaster will play Hansel. I'd suggest no funny business."

That night, Ginger didn't get a wink of sleep. Her eyes ached as she dragged herself to the Castleteria the next morning and mumbled her breakfast order: three little candied bacon cupcakes with Maple SyrUp-on a Time ice cream in a Wonderland waffle cone.

Hagatha grunted, and bounced two scoopfuls of watery scrambled eggs on top of rubbery sausage patties. "*NEXT!*"

Ginger sat at the table in the farthest corner and began seasoning her breakfast. Seasoning

food always helped take her mind off things. But Ginger couldn't forget about the retest. She didn't want to be a villain, but she *did* want to cook. And Ginger knew that if she failed, she might never get to cook again.

Over the next several days, Ginger baked enough desserts to feed a giant. But at the end of each day, she always seemed to be a few treats short. She thought someone must have been snacking behind her back. So on the fourth day, Ginger cooked hextra-sticky buns. They were cinnamony, gooey, and had a spell that made the person who ate them stick in place.

As soon as the first batch was set to cool, Ginger heard someone holler, "Hey! Let go!"

"Gotcha!" Ginger shouted as she spun around. "Cerise?"

Cerise Hood, the daughter of Little Red Riding Hood, was stuck to the pastry. "Sorry; it just smelled so good. I didn't think you'd miss one or two."

"Or three or four or ten," Ginger said, laughing as she reached into the cooler for an unfreeze pop. She wasn't upset her friend had been sneaking desserts. Cerise devoured the pop and slowly unfroze.

"Say, these are great. What kind of spell did you put on these to make them so delicious?" Cerise asked, admiring the chocolate doughnuts.

"They're just regular doughnuts," Ginger said. "People just can't get enough." Then Ginger had an idea! She knew just what to do to complete her fairytale without being a villain.

Later that week, Ginger was as cool as an ever-chill mint for her retest. She played her part just as it was written. She trapped "Hansel" in a cage, and shackled "Gretel" to the wall. Then it was time to put her plan into action.

"You must eat, boy!" Ginger said as she slid a tray piled high with doughnuts to Headmaster Grimm, who was pretending to be Hansel.

Playing the part, Headmaster Grimm bit into his first doughnut. "It's quite good actually," he said, slipping out of character. "Is this porridge cream pie? Simply delicious! I must have the recipe!"

Before too long, Headmaster Grimm devoured the entire tray. Ginger slid him another. And another. The headmaster couldn't stop himself!

He ate all the desserts, just as Hansel was supposed to in Ginger's fairytale. He was stuffed, but happy. Madam Baba Yaga announced that Ginger had done her part and passed her hexam.

"That was some trick you pulled. What kind of sorcery did you use? Some kind of ever-eating spell?" Madam Baba Yaga asked as one eyeball widened.

"No sorcery," Ginger replied. "I don't want to be a villain. I hoped that if Headmaster Grimm loved what I baked, he just might let me tell a new story."

That night, in the Throne Economics room, Ginger hosted her first MirrorCast.

"Welcome to Spells Kitchen, where the secret ingredient to happiness is good food," she said cheerfully into the camera. "On today's episode, we're making doughnuts."

Farrah Goodfairy

Outside the Magicology classroom, laughter filled the halls of the school. Inside the room, however, Farrah Goodfairy, the daughter of the Fairy Godmother from Cinderella's story, was nervously meeting with the Three Fairies Council.

For months, Farrah had worked on the most important test that every Fairy Godmother must pass—the Cinderella Ball Gown and Glass Slipper test.

She'd personally selected her creative team: Wonderland's future Queen of Hearts, Lizzie Hearts, who had a knack for designing dresses; and Cedar Wood, Pinocchio's daughter, who was the most talented painter in school.

Now the Three Fairies were concerned about Farrah's fairytale progress. They'd heard that Ashlynn Ella, the daughter of Cinderella, had fallen in love with Hunter, the son of the Hunstman. They told Farrah that if Ashlynn did not fall in love with a Prince Charming, there would be no Cinderella, and Farrah would disappear.

POOF

Now it was up to Farrah to fix her fairytale.

Back in her room, the Three Fairies' words echoed in Farrah's head. "What am I going to do?" she said. Her head dropped on her desk. Farrah wanted to tell Ashlynn that if she chose Hunter instead of a Prince Charming, they might both disappear. But she couldn't ask a friend to make a choice like that. This was something she had to figure out on her own.

It was hard for Farrah to hocus focus with the possibility of disappearing hanging over her wings. But she had to. The final outfit for her hexam was finally finished and ready to be photographed for her MirrorBlog.

The centerpiece of Farrah's design was a twist on Cinderella's classic glass slippers. Cedar had hand-painted the entire Cinderella story on the slippers, making them hextra special.

"Oh, Cedar!" Farrah exclaimed when Cedar arrived with the shoes. "They're perfect!" Fairy gently, Farrah picked up the shoes.

Just as Farrah went to place the glass slippers next to the gown she'd designed, Lizzie came into the room, slamming the door a little too hard behind her. Farrah dropped the shoes in surprise and they fell to the floor, shattering.

Cedar, Lizzie, and Farrah stood frozen in shock. They were speechless.

"Aces and jacks, no!" Lizzie said. "I'm so sorry, Farrah."

"It's okay, Lizzie," Farrah replied. "These things happen." Farrah tapped the shattered slippers with her wand, and they came back together. But the hand-painted art was gone. The spell could not restore that.

"What are we going to do?" cried Cedar. There isn't enough time to start over!"

Farrah sighed. "I think I need to clear my head. I'll talk to you guys later." She left the room just as the Hickory-Dickory-Dock-Clock struck midnight.

Flying through the Enchanted Forest helped
Farrah think. She thought maybe she could just
conjure a plain pair
of glass slippers.
If Ashlynn and
Hunter were still
a couple, she'd
disappear and none of
this would matter anyway. The
next thing Farrah knew, the sun
peeked through the trees. She'd
completely lost track of time!
Farrah flew back to school
as fast as her wings would
carry her, darting over
bushes, around
trees, and under logs.
Suddenly, she slammed
into something.

Or rather, some*one*. Farrah had flown right into Hunter. She apologized: "I should watch where I'm flying. Are you okay, Hunter?"

Hunter Huntsman stood up gingerly and swayed dizzily. "I'm fine," he assured her. "It's nothing compared to the catapults in Hero Training. Where are you off to?"

"Oh, I've got to finish my fairy godmother project," she hexplained.

"Oh, Ashlynn's story," he said, looking down at his feet. "She's kind of been acting weird lately. I keep telling her, I might not be royalty, but we're destined to be together."

He kicked a rock with his raggedy boot. Looking at his boot, Farrah finally had an idea that would fix the whole fairytale mess!

"Hunter, you're a genius! Follow me!" she said, flying as fast as she could toward the school.

Like true friends forever, Cedar and Lizzie helped Farrah until the stroke of midnight before the presentation. They wished her luck as she made her way toward the Charmitorium stage and the waiting Three Fairy Council.

When it was Farrah's turn, Ashlynn stepped from behind the curtain, wearing ash-covered clothes, just like from the beginning of their story. The Council hexpected Farrah to tap Ashlynn with her wand and magically change her clothes into Farrah's spellbinding design. But Farrah had a different idea in mind.

Hunter walked onto the stage and stood next to Ashlynn. The Three Fairies murmured nervously to one another, unsure of what to hexpect. Farrah waved her wand and tapped Hunter on the head.

Hunter's woodsman outfit changed into a
classic royal suit, complete with a noble coat-of-
arms and a pair of black, glass boots. He looked
just like a prince.

Farrah told the Three Fairy Council that this
was her solution to Ashlynn falling in love with
Hunter instead of a Prince Charming.

"Cinderella is about two people who live Happily Ever After, even though they aren't supposed to be together," Farrah said. "I'm just making a few alterations. This story isn't going anywhere."

One of the fairies held up her hand. She cracked a small smile. "Well done," she said at last.

Farrah had passed the Fairy Godmother test!

Farrah's wings lifted her off the ground! Ashlynn and Hunter still could have a Happily Ever After, and Farrah was there to stay, no matter what.

Duchess Swan

Before Princessology class began, all the other girls flocked together to chitchat about boys and parties while Duchess Swan pored over her notes. The midterm hexams were only a few weeks away, and Duchess knew it took a lot of hocus focus to be the top princess in school.

After the bell rang, their teacher, Mrs. Her Majesty the White Queen, glided into the room and began class. She hexplained that for their midterm hexams, the students would be graded on their ability to inspire people with their Happily Ever Afters.

Duchess grew worried. Her fairytale, Swan Lake, didn't have a Happily Ever After. In fact, when it was Duchess's turn to be the White Swan, her story was destined to have a tragic ending in which she would be cursed into the body of a swan.

After class, Duchess asked her teacher how she could inspire others with her Happily Ever After if she didn't have one. She recounted her fairytale for Mrs. Her Majesty the White Queen, explaining that it was actually a ballet called *Swan Lake*. In the story, Duchess was a princess who was cursed into a swan's body by an evil wizard. Her Prince Charming would fall in love with her and promise to break the spell. But, instead of having a Happily Ever After, the prince would be tricked into falling in love with the wizard's daughter, the Black Swan.

Tears began rolling down Duchess's cheeks as she thought of her tragic ending.

"Oh, I see," Mrs. Her Majesty the White Queen said, laying her hand over her heart. "But no matter how your story ends, the assignment is still to inspire your audience. Inspiration is the key to a Happily Ever After."

Duchess thought that inspiring her audience was the least of her worries. She was sure everyone loved her! But she also knew it would take some work. Duchess's story wasn't as popular as Apple White's or Ashlynn Ella's. But still, Duchess thought she was the most graceful, most talented princess in Ever After High! She was sure it was only a matter of time before everyone flocked to her.

But Duchess couldn't find fans anywhere in the Village of Book End. "Hey, you!" she called out. "I'm performing my ballet, the story of the Swan Queen! You and your son should come."

"You mean my daughter?" the ogre lady said, upset Duchess had assumed her daughter was a boy. She grabbed her daughter's arm and stomped away.

"Like it matters," Duchess grumbled under her breath. She was too annoyed to be polite. "What about you, sir?" she said to a man sitting near her, reading a book. "Come see my fairytale, Swan Lake! It's not like you have anything better to do."

The man looked just as upset as the ogre lady. "You're very rude, young lady! This isn't how to get fans," he said to Duchess as he stormed away. But instead of listening, Duchess just became more annoyed.

Hmmph! she thought. Duchess couldn't believe no one wanted to come to her show, or that a stranger thought she was rude. But after a moment, Duchess started to think. She'd upset the ogre lady and the man with the book. Then she remembered how in Princessology, all the other girls would chat before class, and never included Duchess.

Duchess knew that the White Swan wasn't supposed to be rude. But maybe everyone was right…and Duchess hadn't been fairy nice.

Luckily, there was one person Duchess could go to for honesty: Faybelle Thorn, daughter of the Dark Fairy. Faybelle's destiny was to be a villain, and she royally embraced the role.

When Duchess arrived at Faybelle's room, she asked her for the truth. "Faybelle, am I an awful person?" she asked.

"Oh godmother, no," Faybelle responded. "Why would you ever think that?"

"Nobody wants to see my midterm hexam performance," Duchess explained. "People think I say rude things. But that doesn't make any sense. I'm the next White Swan."

Faybelle thought for a moment before answering. "Duchess, maybe really you're the next Black Swan."

Duchess was upset. She was the princess in her story—not the villain!

Faybelle hexplained that the White Swan was supposed to be humble, modest, and vulnerable. The Black Swan wasn't.

Duchess worried that Faybelle was right—
perhaps she was a villain at heart. But then,
she realized she could take back control of this
fairytale. It was time to set the story straight.
Duchess had to rediscover her White Swan side.

The White Swan is humble. Duchess had to swallow her pride and admit her mistakes. So Duchess went back into the Village of Book End to find the ogre lady and the man with the book. She apologized to both of them and offered them front-row seats to her performance if they were interested in coming.

The White Swan is modest. Duchess had to earn her fans if she wanted anyone to come to her performance, so it was time for her to be nice and polite to everyone. So, as she walked around Book End, she spoke about her story modestly.

"Hexcuse me, I'm performing my fairytale for my midterm hexam," she said politely as people passed by. "Though you might not know my story fairy well, I think you will find it moving." People seemed a lot more interested than last time.

The White Swan is vulnerable. On the night of midterm hexams, Duchess danced her true heart out. During the tragic ending, there wasn't a dry eye in the house. The crowd erupted in a standing ovation! The stage flooded with flower bouquets! Duchess had done it! She inspired her fans. They loved her. Duchess's tragedy had become a Happily Ever After.

Darling Charming

The "Charming" family name came with a lot of hexpectations. Many fairytales had a Prince Charming who saved the day, and one day Daring and Dexter Charming would be heroes in their own fairytales. But their little sister, Darling Charming, didn't know of any story for the *daughter* of King Charming.

Since Darling was a Charming, Headmaster Grimm "just happened" to discover a nearly forgotten fairytale called "Princess Charming" and declared it Darling's destiny. Darling was pretty sure he made it up. There was only one problem: The story required her to be a damsel-in-distress. But Darling wanted to be a hero!

One day, Darling was out with her brother, Daring, trying on a glamorous ball gown she would wear for Spring Fairest. While she was being fitted in the dress shop, Darling looked at the gown her mother had picked out. It was spellbinding, but Darling wondered how she was going to be able to play the Fairest Games. Still, she'd wear it to make her family happy.

Darling thanked the seamstress for helping with her dress and followed Daring out of the shop. Suddenly, a flier with a picture of a sad-looking ogre was put in her hands.

"Bring back Rugsy!" shouted Rosabella Beauty, daughter of Beauty and the Beast, as she handed a flier to everyone who passed by. "He was unjustly kicked out of school. Being an ogre is not a crime!"

"Rescue an ogre?" Daring said as he doubled over with laughter. Darling's heart broke for Rugsy. Some Charming needed to help, and it obviously wasn't going to be Daring.

Darling had a feeling her other brother, Dexter, might want to help the ogre. They had always understood each other, and she was sure he'd join this just cause.

Darling found Dexter slumping against his locker. He had a quill and paper in one hand, and a picture of Raven Queen, the good-hearted daughter of the Evil Queen, in the other. He'd had a crush on her for a while.

Darling sat down next to him. "You okay?" she asked.

Dexter sighed. "I can't find the right words to tell Raven how I feel." He buried his face into the paper as he crossed out and rewrote a poem a few times over.

Darling could tell he was too distracted to help. It was time for Plan B. If Dexter couldn't help her, she hoped that Raven could.

Darling found Raven in her room and hexplained that she wanted to help Rugsy the ogre. She wanted Raven to teleport her to the ogre so she could help bring him back to school.

Raven tapped her chin thoughtfully. "I've got to warn you," she said at last. "My magic can backfire when I use it to help people. You still want to go through with this?"

Without any hesitation, Darling nodded. She couldn't just leave Rugsy when he needed her help!

As Raven began casting her spell, things around Darling started glowing purple. She was filled with a warm, fuzzy feeling. It was working! Suddenly, the world started shaking. A loud buzzing sound rose to a piercing shriek.

The next moment, Darling was in total darkness. The air was stuffy and stale. She started shivering.

"Hello?" she called out.

"Hello?" a deeper, hoarse voice shouted. "Is somebody there?"

"Where are you?" Darling yelled back. She followed the voice as she ducked under low stone ceilings, squeezed through tight passageways, and balanced across narrow bridges. Finally, the voice was nearby. *This must be it*, she thought. Turning the corner, she expected to find Rugsy.

Only instead it was a knight in white armor, stuck halfway through the wall.

"Please help," he called. Without a second thought, Darling backed up, launched herself from the wall, and threw her entire bodyweight into him.

"I'm almost unstuck," he said with hope. "Run faster!"

"I can't run faster. But…" She snapped her fingers. Every Charming had a special magic touch. When she flipped her hair, everything slowed down. Everything, that is, hexcept her.

Backing up against the wall, she flung her hair back. Time slowed to a crawl. She pushed hard off the wall. The wind pressed against her face. She lowered her shoulder, and slammed into the knight. With that, he fell through to the other side. And she fell through with him.

And fell. And fell. And fell.

The ground grew closer in a hurry. There was only one thing she could do. She grabbed the White Knight, turned against the wind, ducked her head down, and flipped her hair. The world slowed down just enough to land safely on the ground.

They were surrounded by an overgrown forest like she'd never seen. Trees had rainbow-colored spiral patterns. Flowers nearly thrust themselves out of their roots to grab them.

"Where are we?" Darling asked, kicking away a thorny vine that tried to wrap around her ankle.

"Wonderland," the White Knight answered as he entered the dense woods.

Darling had heard about the madness that had taken over Wonderland when the Evil Queen tried to rule it.

With a swing of his sword, the White Knight cleared a wall of thorns, revealing a wooden door. "Ah, here we are," he said, pulling a key from his belt. He unlocked the door, and it swung open with a creak.

"Well, come inside. It's only my house," the White Knight said as Darling eyed the door curiously.

The exhausted, grizzled White Knight sunk into his lounge chair, savoring the comfort.

"How did you get stuck, anyway?" Darling asked as she took a seat across from him.

"After they captured the Evil Queen, I helped many people escape," he explained. "I was the last one through the gate. I thought I'd jumped just in time, but then it closed on top of me. I was trapped for ages. Thank you for saving me." He smiled gratefully at Darling.

"Would you mind showing me the way back to Ever After?" Darling asked.

"You're a true hero," the White Knight answered confidently. "You'll find a way."

Darling stared at his armor, still shining like brand-new. Her reflection stared back, and she knew her destiny. She really was a hero, and now it was time to fight for her own Once Upon a Time.